LONG, BROAD & QUICKEYE

LONG, BROAD & QUICKEYE

ADAPTED AND ILLUSTRATED BY

EVALINE NESS

Charles Scribner's Sons   New York

Printed in the United States of America
Library of Congress Catalog Card Number 69-17060

To Nancy Q. who . . .

Once upon a time there lived a king who had an only son whom he loved dearly. Now one day the king sent for his son and said to him: "My dearest child, my hair is gray and I am old, and soon I shall feel no more the warmth of the sun or look upon the trees and flowers. But before I die, I should like to see you with a good wife; therefore marry, my son, as speedily as possible."

"Father," replied the prince, "now and always, I ask nothing better than to do your bidding, but I know of no one that I want to marry."

The old king drew from his pocket a key of gold and gave it to his son, saying, "Go up the staircase, right up to the top of the tower. Look carefully around you, and then come and tell me what you like best of all that you see."

The prince had never before been in the tower, so he had no idea what it might contain. He started climbing.

The staircase wound around and around until the prince was almost giddy, but he had been told to go to the top, and to the top he went. There he found himself in a hall that had an iron door at one end. This door he unlocked with his golden key and passed through into a vast chamber which had a ceiling sprinkled with stars and a carpet of silk soft as turf. Twelve windows let in the light of the sun, and on every window was painted the figure of a young girl, each more beautiful than the last. While the prince gazed at them in surprise, not knowing which he liked best, the girls lifted their eyes and smiled at him. He waited, expecting them to speak, but no sound came.

Then he noticed that one of the windows was covered by a curtain. He lifted it and saw before him the image of a maiden beautiful as the day and sad as the tomb. She was clothed in white, with a crown of pearls. The prince gazed at her, entranced, but as he looked, the sadness which was on her face seemed to pass into his heart, and he cried out: "This one shall be my wife. This one and no other."

As he said the words, the young girl blushed and hung her head, and all the other figures vanished.

The young prince went quickly back to his father and told him all he had seen and which girl he had chosen for his wife. The old man listened to him full of sorrow, and then he spoke: "You have done ill, my son, to search out that which was hidden, and you are running to meet a great danger. This young girl has fallen into the power of a wicked wizard, who lives in an iron castle. Many young men have tried to rescue her, and none has ever come back. But what is done is done. You have chosen. Go, dare your fate, and return to me safe and sound."

So the prince embraced his father, mounted his horse, and set forth to seek his bride. He rode gaily for several hours, until he found himself in a wood where he had never been before. The thick trees shut out the sun, and soon he had lost his way among the winding paths and deep valleys. He had given up all hope of getting out of this horrible place when a voice called to him: "Hey! Hey! Stop a minute!"

The prince turned and saw a very tall man running toward him.

"My lord," he panted, "take me into your service. If you do, you will never be sorry."

"Who are you?" asked the prince, "and what can you do?"

"Long is my name, and I can lengthen my body at will. Do you see that nest up there on the top of that tree? Well, I can get it for you without climbing the tree." Long stretched himself up and up and up until he was as tall as the tree itself. He put the nest in his pocket, and before you could wink your eyelid he had made himself small again.

"Yes, you know your business," said the prince, "but birds' nests are of no use to me. Now if you were only able to get me out of this wood, you would indeed be good for something."

"Oh, there's no difficulty about that," replied Long. He stretched himself up and up and up until he was taller than the tallest tree in the forest. He looked all around and said, "That direction is the quickest way out of the wood." Shortening himself again, he took the prince's horse by the bridle and led him along. Very soon they were clear of the forest. Before them spread a wide plain ending in high rocks, and beyond the rocks were mountains covered with trees.

Long turned to the prince and said, "My lord, here comes my comrade. You should take him into your service too, as you will find him a great help."

"Well, call him then, so that I can see what sort of a man he is."

"He is too far off for that," replied Long. "He would hardly hear my voice, and he couldn't be here for some time yet. I think I had better bring him here myself."

This time Long stretched himself to such a height that his head was lost in the clouds. He made two or three strides, took his friend on his back, and set him down before the prince. The new-comer was a very fat man, and as round as a barrel.

"Who are you?" asked the prince, "and what can you do?"

"My lord, Broad is my name, and I can make myself as wide as I please."

"Let me see you do it."

"Run, my lord, as fast as you can, to the wood!" cried Broad. Then he began to swell.

The prince did not understand why he should run to the wood, but when he saw Long flying toward it, he thought he had better follow him. He was only just in time, for Broad had so inflated himself that he covered the plain entirely. You would have thought he was a mountain!

Then Broad drew a deep breath. The whole forest trembled while he shrank to his usual size.

"Well, well," said the prince. "It is not every day one meets a man of your sort. I will take you into my service."

So the three companions started across the plain. When they drew near the rocks, they met a man whose eyes were covered by a bandage.

"Your excellency," said Long, "this is our third comrade. You will do well to take him into your service. I assure you, you will find him worth his salt."

"Who are you?" asked the prince. "And why are your eyes bandaged?"

"My lord, I am forced to bandage my eyes because I see only too well. Without the bandage my eyes pierce through everything. Everything I look at catches fire or falls into a thousand pieces. They call me Quickeye."

And so saying, he took off his bandage and turned toward a rock. As he fixed his eyes upon it, a crack was heard, and in a few minutes the rock became a heap of sand.

"You are a wonderful creature," said the prince. "I would be a fool not to take you into my service. But since your eyes are so good, tell me how far I am from the Iron Castle."

"If you were traveling alone," replied Quickeye, "it would take you at least a year to get to it, but with our help you can arrive there tonight."

"There is a princess in the castle. Do you see her?"

"A wizard keeps her in a high tower, guarded by iron bars."

"Ah, help me to free her!" cried the prince.

And they promised they would.

Then they all set out for the Iron Castle. As the prince's horse raced as fast as the wind, Long strode easily beside him, carrying Broad on one shoulder and Quickeye on the other. The eyes of Quickeye cut gorges through solid rock and dense forests. The highest mountains were flattened to sand to make a path as straight as an arrow to the Iron Castle.

The sun was setting as the companions crossed the iron bridge which led to the courtyard gates. As they entered the courtyard, the bridge lifted and the gates clanged shut behind them.

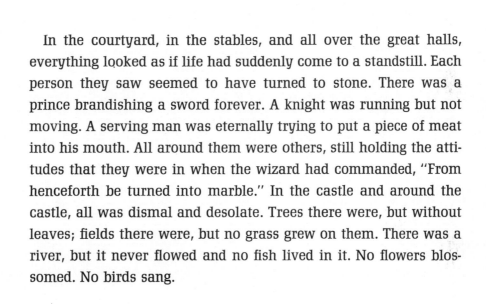

In the courtyard, in the stables, and all over the great halls, everything looked as if life had suddenly come to a standstill. Each person they saw seemed to have turned to stone. There was a prince brandishing a sword forever. A knight was running but not moving. A serving man was eternally trying to put a piece of meat into his mouth. All around them were others, still holding the attitudes that they were in when the wizard had commanded, "From henceforth be turned into marble." In the castle and around the castle, all was dismal and desolate. Trees there were, but without leaves; fields there were, but no grass grew on them. There was a river, but it never flowed and no fish lived in it. No flowers blossomed. No birds sang.

The prince and his friends walked through endless rooms until they reached the dining-hall. It was brilliantly lighted. The table was covered with wine and fruit and was laid for four. They waited, expecting someone to come, but nobody did. Finally they sat down and began to eat and drink, for they were very hungry.

Just as they had finished their supper, the door burst open and the wizard entered the hall. He was old and hump-backed and bald. A gray beard fell to his knees. He wore a black robe and around his waist there were three iron bands. He held the hand of a lady of wonderful beauty, dressed in white, with a crown of pearls. Her face was pale and sad as death itself.

The prince knew her at once. He moved forward eagerly, but the wizard gave him no time to speak: "I know why you are here. Very good. You may have her if for three nights you can prevent her from escaping. If you fail, you and your friends will be turned to stone, like those who came here before you." He turned abruptly and left the hall.

The prince could not take his eyes from the princess, she was so lovely. He talked to her, but she neither answered nor smiled. She sat as if she were made of marble. He seated himself beside her, determined not to close his eyes that night, for fear she would escape.

In order that she should be doubly guarded, Long stretched himself like a strap around the room. Broad took his stand by the door and puffed himself out so that not even a mouse could slip by. Quickeye leaned against a pillar which stood in the middle of the hall. But soon they were all asleep. They slept soundly the whole night long.

In the morning, at the first peep of dawn, the prince awoke with a start. But the princess was gone. He aroused his friends and implored them to tell him what to do.

"Calm yourself, my lord," said Quickeye. "I have found her already. A hundred miles from here is a forest. In the middle of the forest, an old oak, and on the top of the oak, an acorn. That acorn is the princess. If Long will take me on his shoulders, we will soon bring her back." And in less time than it takes to walk around a cottage, they had returned from the forest, and Long presented the acorn to the prince.

"Now, my lord, throw it on the ground."

The prince obeyed and was overjoyed to see the princess appear.

At that moment the door slammed open as before, and the wizard entered with a loud laugh. But when he saw the princess, his face darkened. He growled in fury. Then Cric-Crac! One of the iron bands around his waist gave way with a crash. He seized the princess and dragged her away.

All that day the prince wandered about the castle, looking at the marble men and waiting for nightfall. Three times during the day food appeared, as if by magic, for the prince and his companions. And it was not until supper was ended that the wizard appeared and delivered the princess into the care of the prince.

All four determined that this time they would keep awake at any cost. But it was no use. Off they went as they had done before, and when the prince awoke the next morning, the princess was gone.

With a pang of shame, he rushed to Quickeye. "Wake up! Wake up, Quickeye! Can you see the princess?"

Quickeye rubbed his eyes and answered: "Yes, I see her. Two hundred miles from here there is a mountain. Within this mountain is a rock. In the rock, a precious stone. This stone is the princess. Long shall take me there, and we will be back before you can turn around."

Long took him on his shoulders and they set out. At every stride they covered twenty miles, and as they drew near the mountain, Quickeye fixed his burning eyes upon it. In an instant it split into a thousand pieces, and amid the rubble there sparkled the precious stone. Immediately they brought it to the prince, who flung it down. As the stone touched the floor, the princess stood before him.

When the wizard arrived and saw the princess, his eyes shot forth flames of fury. CRIC-CRAC! And another iron band broke apart. Roaring with rage, he seized the princess and pulled her from the room.

The day passed as the day before. After supper the wizard brought back the princess. He looked the prince straight in the eyes and said, "We shall see which of us two will gain the prize after all!"

That night the four friends struggled harder than ever to keep awake. They even walked about instead of sitting down. But it was quite useless. One after another they fell asleep.

When morning came, the prince awoke first, as usual, and as usual the princess was gone. He shouted to Quickeye: "Get up, get up, Quickeye, and tell me where the princess is!"

Quickeye looked about for some time before answering. "Oh, my lord, she is far, far away. Three hundred miles from here there lies a black sea. At the bottom of the sea there is a shell. In the middle of the shell is fixed a gold ring. That gold ring is the princess. But do not vex your soul. We will get her. But this time Long must take Broad with him. He will be needed."

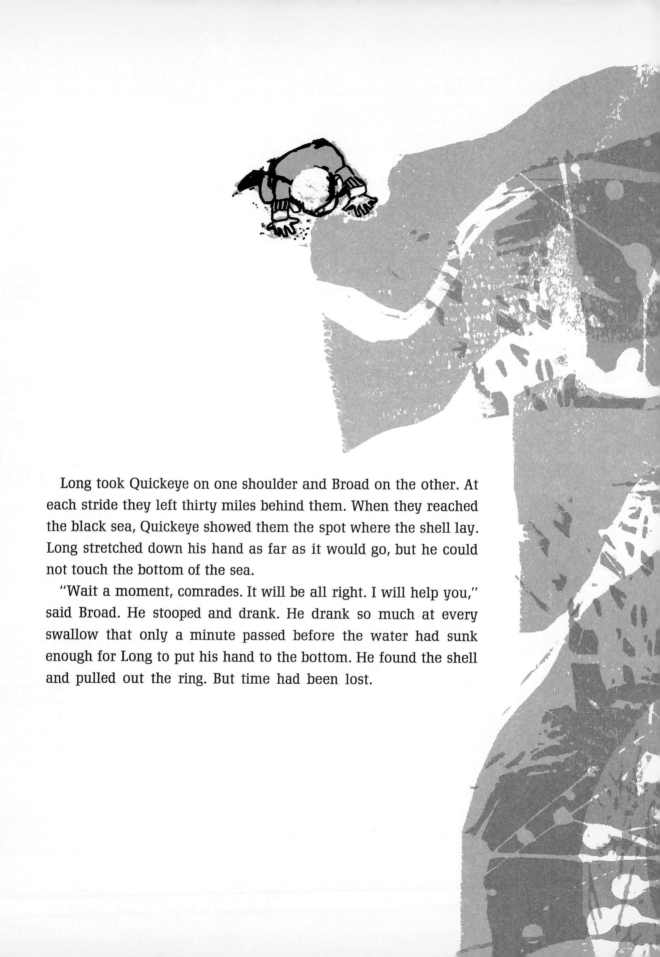

Long took Quickeye on one shoulder and Broad on the other. At each stride they left thirty miles behind them. When they reached the black sea, Quickeye showed them the spot where the shell lay. Long stretched down his hand as far as it would go, but he could not touch the bottom of the sea.

"Wait a moment, comrades. It will be all right. I will help you," said Broad. He stooped and drank. He drank so much at every swallow that only a minute passed before the water had sunk enough for Long to put his hand to the bottom. He found the shell and pulled out the ring. But time had been lost.

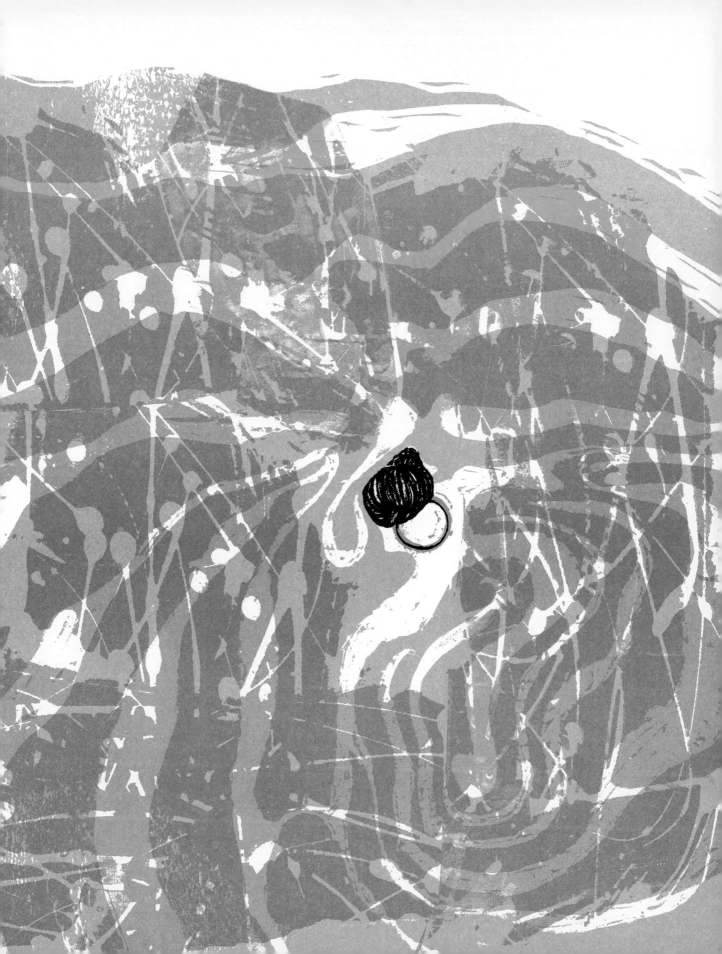

The dawn was breaking fast as they started back to the castle, where the prince was waiting in an agony of fear.

As the first rays of the sun crept over the mountaintops, the wizard appeared. When he found the prince alone, he broke into peals of wicked laughter. But as he laughed, a loud crash was heard. The window splintered into a thousand pieces, a gold ring glittered in the air, then struck the floor. There stood the princess! Miles away, Quickeye had seen the danger that threatened the prince, and Long, with one gigantic effort, had thrown the ring right through the window.

The wizard shrieked and howled with such rage that the whole castle trembled on its foundations. CRIC-CRAC-CRAC! The third iron band split. Where once the wizard had stood, an ugly black bird raised its wings and flew out of the window and vanished.

Then the princess's enchanted silence was broken. Blushing like a rose, she thanked the prince for delivering her.

But it was not only the princess who was restored to life by the flight of the evil wizard. The marble figures became men once more. The horses neighed, the flowers blossomed, birds flew in the air, and fish darted in the water. Everywhere you looked, all was life, all was joy!

The knights who had been turned into stone offered their homage to the prince who had set them free.

"Do not thank me," said the prince, "for I have done nothing. Without my faithful friends, Long, Broad, and Quickeye, *I* would have been one of *you.*"

He then bade them farewell and departed with the princess and his three companions for the kingdom of his father.

The old king wept for joy at the sight of his son and insisted that the wedding should take place as soon as possible.

All the knights of the Iron Castle were invited to the ceremony.

When it was over, Long, Broad, and Quickeye presented themselves
to the prince and princess to say good-bye. The prince begged them
to stay. He offered them all their hearts could desire if they would
only remain with him. But they said that an idle life was not for
them and that they could never be happy unless they were busy.

So Long, Broad, and Quickeye went away to look for more work.

And for all we know, they are helping people still.